SCARY
FAIRY TALES

TOM THUMB
the TINY SPOOK

ORCHARD BOOKS
338 Euston Road, London NW1 3BH
Orchard Books Australia
Level 17/207 Kent Street, Sydney, NSW 2000

First published in 2015 by Orchard Books

ISBN 978 1 40832 968 9

A CIP catalogue record for this book is available
from the British Library.

1 3 5 7 9 10 8 6 4 2
Printed in Great Britain

Orchard Books is a division of Hachette Children's Boo
an Hachette UK company.

www.hachette.co.uk

SERIOUSLY SILLY

SCARY
FAIRY TALES

TOM THUMB
the TINY SPOOK

Laurence Anholt
& Arthur Robins

ORCHARD

www.anholt.co.uk

GOOD EVENING, LADIES AND
GENTLEMEN.

My name is
THE MAN WITHOUT A HEAD.

Of course I have a head really... it's just
that my head is removable. It's been a
very naughty head today, so I've made it
sit in the wastepaper basket.

So, you like SCARY STORIES, do
you? Well, I warn you, the stories I
am about to tell are so TERRIFYING
that grown men have been known to do
wee-wees in their panties.

Perhaps you are the kind of person who
doesn't believe in ghosts? I expect you
think you can see right through them.

This tiny tale may change your mind. It's about a small spook called Tom Thumb, who had a wail of a time.

Are you sitting comfortably, horror-hunters? Then I'll begin.

Tonight's tale is...

TOM THUMB
THE TINY SPOOK...

Once upon a time, there was a big house in the middle of the countryside. It was called Midnight Manor. Nobody went near Midnight Manor. The people in the village thought it was haunted.

The people were quite right, Fans of Fear.

Midnight Manor was haunted by two of the nicest ghosts you could ever hope to meet. Their names were Mr and Mrs White.

Mr and Mrs White were very happy ghosts. They could do whatever they wanted at Midnight Manor – swim in the empty swimming pool or float up and down the banisters.

Only one thing was missing – Mr and Mrs White longed to have a ghostie child to call their own.

"Look at all these empty rooms," wailed Mr White. "Midnight Manor is far too big for two old ghosts."

"How I wish we could have a little ghost to care for," sighed Mrs White. "You know what, Mr White? I wouldn't mind if he was as small as my spooky thumb!"

You may not believe this, Fans of Fear, but Mrs White's wish came true... one evening a small white thing came floating through the keyhole. At first, they thought it was a tiny lost cloud, but when Mrs White put on her spooktecles she realised, to her delight, that it was a ghostly boy no bigger than her thumb.

"What's your name, little spook?" said Mr White.

The little spook hopped onto the kitchen table, danced about on a plate and sang a tiny spooky song.

Tom Thumb, Tom Thumb
Tiny as a stick of gum
Tom Thumb, Tom Thumb
Scary as a witch's bum!

"Oh, isn't he sweet!" sighed Mrs White.

"I don't want to be sweet," said the tiny spook. "I want to be scary like you."

"Well, perhaps you will grow into a big ghost one day," said Mr White. "In the meantime, we love you just the way you are."

So Tom Thumb settled into Midnight Manor with Mr and Mrs White. They gave him all his favourite things to eat – ghoulash and spookghetti followed by ice scream. But he never grew any bigger.

In fact, Tom Thumb was so tiny that Mrs White
made him a sleeping bag out of a sock and a bed
from an old shoe.

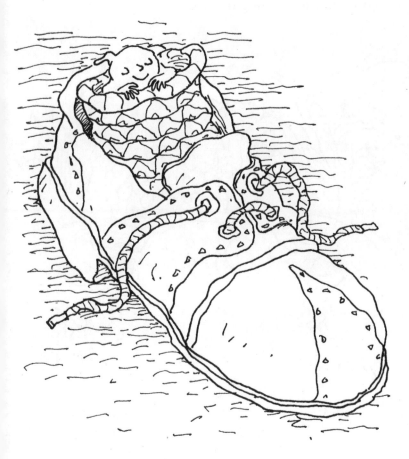

Tom Thumb may have been a tiny spook, but he knew how to make BIG trouble. He was always getting into mischief. One night he rode a frog around the garden. He got so muddy that Mrs White put him in a bubble bath. Then she hung him on the washing line to dry.

Tom's favourite game was Hide and Shriek.
When Mr White sat down to read the spookpaper
(*The Daily Wail*), Tom Thumb would hide between
the pages. Then he would pop up and shout:

When Mrs White was relaxing in the bathtub,
Tom would pop out of the tap shouting:

"Oh, I wish he had some little friends to play with!" sighed Mr and Mrs White. Well, guess what, Fans of Fear? Their wish came true again, as you shall see.

As you know, ghosts stay awake all night, so of course they sleep all day. One morning, Mrs White was tucking Tom Thumb into his shoe, when he asked her a very funny question – "Mum, do you believe in people?"

"Now I don't want you believing in all that scary nonsense," said Mrs White. "I've lived in Midnight Manor for two hundred years and I've never seen a person."

"No," said Mr White, coming into the bedroom. "The boy is right. I did see a person once. One day I couldn't sleep, so I went out in the middle of the light. I floated as far as the village and I saw one of them, plain as day, walking a little dog, he was. I almost jumped out of my sheet. I flew home as fast as I could and that's the last time I went out before dark."

"Don't put silly ideas in the boy's head," said Mrs White. "You'll give him daymares. You go to sleep and forget all that nonsense, Tom Thumb. There's no such thing as people."

But Tom Thumb was a curious spook. He couldn't stop wondering if there really were such things as people.

One foggy evening in mid winter, Mrs White
went into the kitchen and there was Tom Thumb,
standing by the door with a tiny spooksack on
his back.

"Where are you going, Tom?" she asked.
"Thank you for looking after me, Mum,"
said Tom Thumb. "But I'm going off to have an
adventure."

Mrs White was terribly sad. Little white tears ran down her cheeks. But she had always known that one day her tiny boy would float away just as he had come. She made him some ghosty toasty, put a small bottle of evaporated milk in his spooksack and kissed her boy goodbye.

"Don't worry, Mum," said Tom Thumb as he stepped outside. "I'll send you a ghostcard."

When Mr White came downstairs, he could tell that something was wrong. "Why do you look so pale?" he said to Mrs White.

"It was your foolish ideas about people," she wailed. "Now we will never see our tiny son again! He has gone out into the foggy night."

"He'll be mist," said Mr White sadly.

Tom Thumb floated down the lane and through the forest, stopping only to eat the food his mother had made. When it began to get light Tom rested by the side of a path.

Suddenly he heard a strange noise.

PING, PING!

To his amazement, he saw a funny man riding a bicycle. It was the first person he had ever seen.

"He doesn't look scary," said Tom Thumb. "I think I'll have a bit of fun."

He lay very still on the ground. The man stopped his bicycle. "Oh!" he said. "Someone has dropped a nice white handkerchief."

He picked up Tom Thumb and was just about to push him into his pocket, when Tom Thumb shouted:

The man almost jumped out of his skin.

"Hee, hee!" giggled Tom Thumb. "Don't worry.
I'm only a tiny spook."

"You are a very cheeky little ghost," laughed the
funny man. "Luckily I am the head teacher of a
school. I will take you to see the children. They
will love to meet you."

So the funny teacher cycled along the path towards the school with Tom sitting in his top pocket enjoying the view.

Tom Thumb was looking forward to going to school. But when they arrived, he was disappointed. He thought the school would be a lovely big building like Midnight Manor, but this school was tiny and almost tumbling down.

All the children gathered around to look at Tom Thumb. They thought it was very funny to see such a tiny spook.

Of course Tom Thumb started to show off. He danced about and sang his little song.

Tom Thumb, Tom Thumb
Tiny as a stick of gum
Tom Thumb, Tom Thumb
Scary as a witch's bum!

The children laughed and laughed. Then one little girl picked up Tom Thumb and said she would look after him. "You can sit on my desk," she said. "Then you will be able join in the lessons."

So, Tom sat on the little girl's desk at the front of the classroom.

"Now then, Tom Thumb," said the funny
teacher, "how good is your maths?"

"Spooktacular!" said Tom Thumb.

All the children giggled.

"Let me see you do some sums," said the teacher.
"Boo + Boo = Boo booo!" said Tom Thumb.
Then the children laughed even more.

As I have told you, ghosts always sleep in the day. All the sums made Tom feel tired. He looked around on the desk and saw a nice woolly pencil case. He undid the zip and snuggled down inside.

When he woke up, he heard someone crying. Tom peeped out of the pencil case, but the classroom seemed empty. All the children were playing outside. Then Tom saw the funny teacher, looking very miserable.

Tom floated over and sat on his lap. "Why are you so sad?" he said.

"Oh dear, Tom," said the teacher. "Look at my school. The roof is leaking, the heating is broken and we don't have any money to put things right. I'm afraid the school will have to close."

"But where will all the children go?" asked Tom.

"I don't know... boo hoo hoo!" said the teacher.

Just then Tom had a tiny idea. "I know," he said, "you can come to Midnight Manor! My mum and dad have a lovely big garden and a swimming pool and lots of empty rooms."

The funny head teacher was very excited. He put a trailer on the back of his bicycle and loaded up all the desks and chairs. Then the teacher and all the children followed Tom Thumb along the path, through the forest and up the lane to Midnight Manor.

Mr and Mrs White were sitting sadly at the kitchen table. Even though Tom Thumb was so naughty, they missed having him there. Suddenly they heard a funny noise.

PING, PING!

"That sounds like a bicycle bell," said Mr White.

Then they heard another funny noise. "That sounds like children laughing," said Mrs White. The door opened and there was their tiny spook with all his friends.

"Guess what?" said Tom. "People aren't scary at all."

So the funny teacher and Mr and Mrs White turned Midnight Manor into a Spooky School. They taught the children all sorts of useful things, like how to float up the banisters and how to play Hide and Shriek. Every day they sang the school song and Tom Thumb sang loudest of all.

Tom Thumb, Tom Thumb
Tiny as a stick of gum
Tom Thumb, Tom Thumb
Scary as a witch's bum!

And that was the giggly, ghostly tale of Tom Thumb the Tiny Spook. Every word was true. So remember, Fans of Fear, always be polite to your teachers and don't spook until you're spooken to.

Now, if my head has been a good boy, I'll let him out of the wastepaper basket.

SCARY
FAIRY TALES

LAURENCE ANHOLT & ARTHUR ROBINS

COLLECT THEM ALL.

Also available as an ebook